To my family and friends

Sheep, sheep, sheep — I love sheep!

Their wool keeps me warm during
a cold winter storm.

I also count sheep to help me fall asleep.

One by one they jump over the gate,
until it gets very late. And then it
seems, I drift to the land of dreams.

But...what happened one night was quite a
sight, for some of the sheep could not leap!

It started with the carpenter who was building a gate. He locked it and left as he was running late. But oh no, this new gate was too tall, and the sheep were way too small.

As the sheep were coming and going, there was no way of knowing, that the gate that was in the way would change their plans that day.

What would they do? How would they pass? This was a time for ideas, and fast.

A fire broke out across the gate and the firefighter sheep could not be late. So, he turned on the fire hose at full blast and used the water to get across fast.

The Olympian sheep was going to her class and was very worried that she could not pass. But then she found a long branch and pole vaulted across in a flash!

There was the ninja sheep who had to be quiet, for if he made a noise there would be a riot. So, he got down on his belly just in case and crawled through the very small space!

The astronaut sheep thought she was out of luck, when she saw that she was stuck. But then she reached into her pocket and found the key to start her rocket. And in a very fast ride, she launched to the other side!

There was a cyclist sheep who was going for a ride, and could not pass to the other side. Good thing he trained every day, because he went up and down the mountain way!

The veterinarian sheep was on her way to see the animals in her clinic that day. She was riding her horse, who had just completed a jumping course, and with one giant stride they jumped to the other side!

19

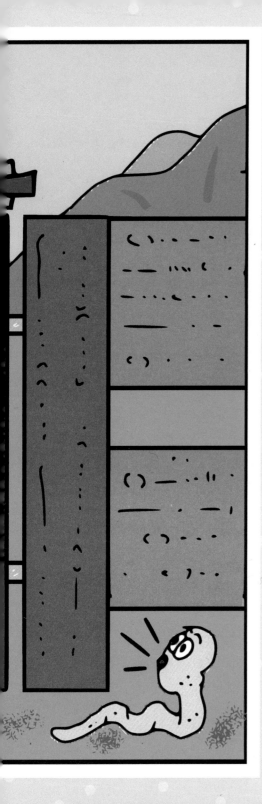

One sheep got a letter in the mail that said a beautiful house was for sale. So, he rushed to the gate that was locked and knocked, and knocked, and knocked. Until the owner heard the sheep's hollers and the sheep bought the house for a thousand dollars!

The architect sheep was worried she would be late, when she arrived at the locked gate. She was carrying the blueprints for her meeting with the Flints. She did not waste any time, and designed a bridge to climb!

The doctor sheep could not leap, for she had worked all night and did not sleep. She spotted a branch with a rope, tied it to her stethoscope, and on the zip-line she went. Although her stethoscope got a little bent...

For all of these sheep it was quite a day, where no sheep could go easily on his or her way. They each had some thinking to do, to creatively get themselves through.

The carpenter sheep came back, and was surprised to see the tracks of all the sheep who were stuck, so he quickly undid the lock.

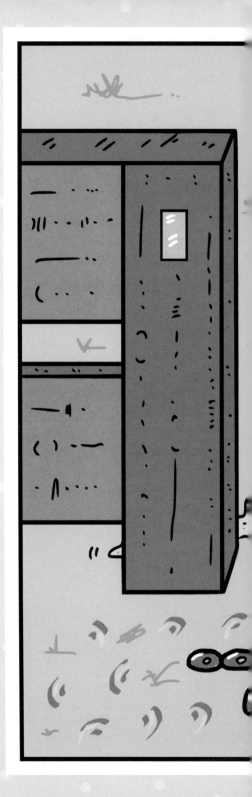

But when the sheep came back they were hoping, that the gate would still not be open. For they had so much fun, and were proud of what they had done.

What happened next was
truly the best.

No sheep would ever be late,
because of a locked gate.

They came up with a plan
that day, to build a place for
all to play.

They built a playground with a swing and a slide, and a tunnel that leads to the other side.

There was a pole and a bridge with a ramp too, it was a fun place with so much to do.

Then one day there was a contest, to see which playground was the best.

Woolytown playground won first prize! It was a wonderful surprise.

The sheep were as proud as could be for making the town happy.

And the sheep of Woolytown could not wait, to go on new adventures beyond the gate.

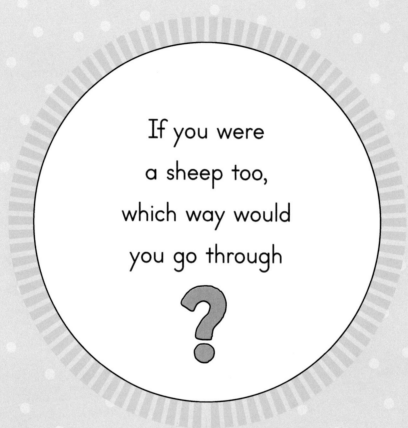

If you were
a sheep too,
which way would
you go through
?

77541848R00022

Made in the USA
Middletown, DE
22 June 2018